For Sarah Louise

First published 1986 by
Lothian Publishing Company Pty. Ltd.
Melbourne, Australia

First published in UK 1986 by
Blackie & Son Ltd.
This edition 1989

British Library Cataloguing in Publication Data

Ingpen, Robert
    The Idle Bear
    1. Title
    823(J)PZ7
ISBN 0 216 92662 9

Blackie and Son Ltd.
7 Leicester Place
London WC2H 7BP

Printed in Hong Kong

Mrs Cunningham

The Idle Bear

Robert Ingpen

Winner 1986 Hans Christian Andersen Medal

Blackie
London

'What kind of a bear are you?'
asked Ted.

'I'm an Idle Bear.'

'But don't you have a name like me?'

'Yes, but my name is Teddy. All bears
like us are called Teddy.'

Ted thought for a while, then said,
'Well, Teddy, I have been
Ted forever—
at least fifty years, I think.'

'Me too,' said Teddy,
'at least that long.'

We could be related, thought Ted
and Teddy together.

'We are related!' announced Ted,
pretending he had known for ages.

'How can you tell, Ted?'
challenged Teddy,
'How do you know?'

'Oh, I just know. Everybody has
relations, I think especially where
I come from,' said Ted
beginning to wish it
wasn't so.

'Where do you come from, Ted?'

'From an idea,' said Ted definitely.

'But ideas are not real, they are only made up,' said Teddy. 'You have to come from somewhere real to have realitives.'

'Not realitives, relatives!' said Ted trying to hide his confusion.

Ted remembered that everybody he
had met had come from 'up the street',
and said, 'I come from up the street.'

'What street?' questioned Teddy.

In desperation Ted said,
'Up the street next to your street.'

'What happens up the street?'

'That depends,' said Ted, now really
confused, 'That depends on
everything else that happens.'
That should do, thought Ted.

'Like what?' demanded Teddy.

Ted tried to remember. 'When I was young,' he began, 'I used to have a lot to do.
I was as important as a bear can be,' Ted paused, then went on,
'later I was put away, and taken out, and put away, and taken out, and put . . .

'Put away where?' interrupted Teddy.

'In a box.'

'What sort of a box? A bear box?'

'I don't know,' said Ted, 'just a box.'

'Oh,' said Teddy.

'Have you got a growl?' said Ted.

'I used to have one but it wore out,' said Teddy.

'Mine still works,' said Ted proudly, 'at least I think it does.'

'Don't you know?'

'That depends,' said Ted, 'that depends on what I do. If I stand like this it works sometimes.'

Ted stood on his head as best he could.

Then he bent backwards.

'It's something to do with my tummy,
 but I've never seen it,' Ted said
 and stood on his head again.

'It's a very small growl, Ted,'
 said Teddy.

'It's better than a worn out growl,'
 said Ted
feeling challenged again.
'It used to be very loud.
 I used to be full of growl
 when I was young,
 up the street.'

'I'm full of straw,' announced Teddy.

Ted ignored that. It sounded
reasonable and anyhow he was
probably full of straw too, if they
were related. But then scarecrows
and cushions are full of straw and
the thought of being related to
a cushion annoyed him.

Ted was still thinking about cushions
and scarecrows when
Teddy startled him by saying,
'Dogs.'

'What about dogs?' said Ted.

'Dogs come from up the street,'
announced Teddy.

Ted thought, *of course they do,*
and remembered Michael.
He hadn't seen Michael for how long?
'It must be forty years,'
thought Ted aloud.

'What?' said Teddy.

'It must be forty years since
I've seen Michael,
I wonder where he is?'

'Michael who?'

'Michael Wood, the dog next door,
up the street.'

'Oh,' said Teddy.

'Why do you wear that bandage?'
asked Teddy.

Ted looked sadly at his bandaged wrist.
'Oh, just because my paw wore out,'
he said.

'Like my growl wore out, I suppose,'
suggested Teddy, glad that Ted
was not perfect.

'I suppose,' said Ted still searching
for a clever reply.
Then he had an idea.

'It gives me a worldly look,'
he explained.

'What does?' demanded Teddy.

'My bandage on my worn out paw,'
  said Ted.
'With that and me together,' he went on,
'I am a Worldly Bear.' He remembered
  that somebody once had admired him,
  and shaken him, and told him he was
  a worldly bear.

'What's a worldly bear?' asked Teddy.

'One that's worldly,' said Ted wisely.
  He was quite content just being
  worldly without having to explain
  what it meant—
  that's part of being worldly.

'I'm an Idle Bear,' said Teddy.

'I know,' said Ted, 'You told me so.'

'Don't you want to know
 What an Idle is?'

'No,' said Ted.

'My owner is an Idle,' said Teddy
 ignoring Ted, 'so I'm an Idle too.'

Ted wished he knew what
an Idle was.

And he is still thinking about it.